D0581217

AT TROWSER'S DOWN

700037466007

NIGHTMARE
AT TROWSER'S DOWN

Michael Cox
Illustrated by Cathy Brett

A & C Black • London

First published 2010 by
A & C Black Publishers Ltd
36 Soho Square, London, W1D 3QY

www.acblack.com

ISBN: 978-1-4081-1334-9

A CIP catalogue for this book is available from the British Library.

This book is produced using paper that is made from wood grown in
managed, sustainable forests. It is natural, renewable and recyclable.
The logging and manufacturing processes conform to the
environmental regulations of the country of origin.

Printed and bound in Great Britain
by J F Print, Sparkford, Somerset

CHAPTER ONE

Thirteen-year-old Tiffany Trotter had just finished writing a text when she heard a deafening roar in the street outside. Looking out of her bedroom window, she saw an enormous red motorbike screech to a halt in front of her house. A moment later, the man who would soon be bringing untold chaos to the lives of the Trotter family leapt from the massive machine.

Almost without thinking, Tiffany pressed 'send' on her mobile, whizzing the text to Julian Butternut, her boyfriend:

```
Darling Sherbert Fountain, miss you
loads. And it's only been 3 hours.
Can't wait to see you again! Fizzy
Pips XXX
```

Then, spellbound by the stranger's appearance, she watched him stride to their front door.

The man was dressed in a jet-black polo-neck, skin-tight black moleskin jeans, scarlet leather boots, and a huge crimson cape that looked as if it had been made from reptile skin. He was extremely tall and thin, with talon-like hands, a large hooked nose and piercing green eyes half-hidden by thick bushy eyebrows. His long straggly hair was streaked with grey and slicked back over his skeleton-like skull.

All of which made Tiffany think of a huge bird of prey. It wouldn't have surprised her if the man had suddenly flapped his arms and soared skywards, then swooped on some unsuspecting pet cat or dog just seconds later, tearing them to pieces.

But he didn't. Ignoring the Trotters' bell, he rapped on the door so hard that the whole house rattled. Tiffany rushed to the stairs just in time to see her dad, Dr Thomas Trotter, open the door.

'Dr Twotter, I pwesume?' cried the stranger.

Then, as Tiffany's dad nodded a polite but wary 'yes', the man thrust out one of his leather-clad talons, grasped Dr Trotter by the hand, and pumped it furiously, barking, 'Allow me to intwoduce myself. Perfidious is the name! Pwofessor Pewegwine Perfidious. I have been twying to find you for many years, Dr Twotter. You come highly wecommended.

Highly wecommended. Oh, I am overjoyed to finally meet you!'

Then he wrapped his arms around Tiffany's dad so tightly that he actually disappeared inside the folds of the stranger's enormous cape. For a few seconds, all that could be seen of Dr Trotter were his feet, kicking frantically.

'Please put me down, Professor Perfidious,' he whimpered. 'I think I am about to expire!'

The professor reluctantly released Dr Trotter and turned his attention to the rest of the family. Immediately, his eyes lit upon Tiffany's four-year-old brother, Toby, who was currently struggling with a rather disturbing vampire fixation.

Without warning, Professor Perfidious gave a dramatic swirl of his enormous cape and rushed at little Toby, crying, 'Oh, vot a pwetty little child! Wavishing! Wavishing!' Then he swept up the boy in his arms and held him high in the air.

This of course caused Toby to go wide-eyed with terror and scream, convinced that this undead lookalike was about to sink his 'fangs' into him.

Somewhat put out by this reaction, the professor immediately thrust the boy into Mrs Trotter's arms, saying, 'Oh dear, I seem to have fwightened him!' But then, a look of sadness crossed his face, as he added, 'Not having any little ones of my own, I am not used to such things.'

After apologies had been made all round, Mrs Trotter took the howling Toby upstairs for a bedtime story. Then Professor Perfidious whisked Tiffany's dad into the study so that they could talk business.

Ten minutes later, the two men emerged, grinning furiously.

The delighted professor gave Dr Trotter a hearty slap on the back and roared, 'I knew you would agwee, Twotter. And I assure you, your new labowatwy will be the best that money can buy. But now I must wace. Lots to do… Cawwots to impwove, waspberries to wefine, wabbits to wevamp, that sort of thing…'

Then Professor Perfidious took his leave, leaping onto his motorbike and roaring off in a cloud of exhaust fumes and startled garden birds.

'Wow!' said Mrs Trotter. 'What was all *that* about?'

'IFARTFASTA!' said Dr Trotter, still grinning from ear to ear.

'Oh, do you now, Tom?' said Mrs Trotter, assuming her husband had just flipped his lid.

'I … FART … FASTA!' repeated Dr Trotter, with a straight face.

'I'm going to work for Professor Perfidious at IFARTFASTA! You know, the Institute For Associated Research Technology Farming Agrobiology Special Task-force Agency!' And when Mrs Trotter still looked puzzled, he said, 'He's just offered me a huge amount of money to give up my job at the university and go and be one of his top research scientists there. Along

9

with the world-famous Dr Pamela Redbridge, I'm to head a crack team of boffins working on a genetics and cloning project so important that it will revolutionise the production of farm animals and crops the world over. It's the best thing that's ever happened to us!'

How *wrong* he would turn out to be...

CHAPTER TWO

Two weeks later, Tiffany's dad started his new job, and his daily routine soon became so familiar it felt like he'd been working for Professor Perfidious for years. Each morning he kissed Mrs Trotter, Tiffany and Toby goodbye, then drove the 80 miles from their home in St Bartholomew's Bottom to Trowser's Down, a bleak and lonely stretch of countryside that was home to the huge complex of laboratories, rabbit hutches, blood banks, organ warehouses, chicken coops, aquaculture vats, and transmutation chambers known as IFARTFASTA.

The moment Dr Trotter arrived at the complex, he put on his spotty bow tie, his long white coat and his thick-rimmed spectacles and headed for the security check-in. Here, Zoltan, Cholera and Pancreas, Professor Perfidious's extremely scary-looking security guards, carefully checked his ID before letting him inside.

Then, holed up in his laboratory, surrounded by beakers bubbling with bacterial gloop, test tubes teeming with tissue cultures and petri dishes pulsating with peptides, he'd work frenziedly to come up with the crucial formulae necessary for the success of Professor Perfidious's 'gweat pwoject'.

Peering into aquaculture vats alive with antibodies, not to mention millions of pink, wiggly tadpole things, he'd add a dash of this, a sprinkle of that and a generous handful of who-knows-what, so that the magical *fusings*, which only he and Dr Redbridge had the expertise to bring about, would take place.

And sometimes, actually *forgetting* that he was in his lab, and not at home preparing spaghetti bolognese, Dr Trotter would absentmindedly *taste* a spoonful of the multi-coloured gloop that foamed and churned in front of him! Which may help to explain some of the remarkable changes to his body that Dr Trotter had begun to notice in the shower. Changes which he took great care to keep secret from the rest of his family...

Tiffany and her mum may not have been aware of *those* changes but, as the weeks passed, they did begin to notice *other* sorts of changes in Dr Trotter. The sparkle disappeared from his once-cheerful eyes. He often looked tired. And, sometimes, he appeared nervous and jumpy.

'Everything all right, dear?' said Mrs Trotter, as they all sat down to dinner one evening.

'Yes, thank you, Mary,' said Dr Trotter. 'Why do you ask?'

'Just wondered,' said Mrs Trotter, patting his hand affectionately. 'And what about Professor Perfidious, are you two still getting on like a house on fire?'

'Well,' said Dr Trotter, suddenly looking tense. 'If I'm honest, he is beginning to make a lot of demands on myself and Pamela. Things we never expected to do. You know, new, er, *challenges*!"

'What sort of *challenges*, Dad?' said Tiffany.

'I'd prefer not to say,' replied Dr Trotter.

'Well, Thomas!' laughed Mrs Trotter, always one to look on the bright side. 'I suppose you should feel flattered. After all, you and Pamela are the only people in the world who can perform these scientific miracles. And think of all the good things your new job is bringing us, like our fabulous home cinema TV system!'

'And Marbles, my lovely pony,' added Tiffany with a huge grin.

But a few weeks later, Dr Trotter arrived home from work looking very worried indeed.

'What is it, darling?' said Mrs Trotter.

'You'll never believe it, Mary!' he said. 'The Redbridges have ... *disappeared*!'

'No!' gasped Mrs Trotter. 'Surely not?'

'Yes, really,' said Dr Trotter. 'Yesterday, they were all at home celebrating their son Nigel's fifteenth birthday. And now they're gone!'

'Where?' asked Tiffany, who had overheard the conversation.

'I've no idea!' said Dr Trotter. 'Only a couple of days ago Pam was showing me the golf clubs they were going to give Nigel as a present. Everything seemed so normal.' He gave a bitter laugh and added, 'Well, as normal as they can be these days at IFARTFASTA!'

'This must be so upsetting for you,' said Mrs Trotter, putting a comforting arm around her husband's shoulders.

'It certainly is,' said Dr Trotter. 'With Pam gone, my workload is going to double!'

These revelations left Mrs Trotter and Tiffany feeling very worried. But not nearly as worried as they would have been had Dr Trotter told them about the rumours that were currently flying around IFARTFASTA. Like the one that claimed just a few days before she and her family had vanished, Dr Redbridge had had a huge row with Professor Perfidious. A row that had ended with Dr Redbridge emptying her test tubes on the floor, then stamping on their contents while yelling, 'You're a monster, Perfidious! I will no longer be part of your foul and freakish Frankenstein schemes!' And that the day after this, someone from Trowser's Down village had said they'd seen Zoltan, Cholera and Pancreas bundling the Redbridges out of their house and into the back of a very rusty old black van, and driving them off in the direction of IFARTFASTA.

Of course, sensible people quickly dismissed these tales as nothing more than tittle-tattle put about by gossips and village idiots, of which Trowser's Down had more than its fair share. But Dr Trotter soon had good reason to believe otherwise…

CHAPTER THREE

'Look here, Twotter,' said Professor Perfidious, handing Dr Trotter a postcard of two kangaroos standing outside the Sydney Opera House. 'This pwoves that Dr Wedbwidge weally has wun off.'

Dr Trotter studied the postcard's Australian stamp and postmark then reread the final part of the message:

Yes, our urge to 'bond' with the wombats and koala bears of this great continent was so strong that my family and I had no choice but catch the first available flight out here. I do hope we haven't caused you too much inconvenience.

Best wishes, Dr Pamela Redbridge

'I will be circulating a copy of this to all employees of IFARTFASTA, the local authowities and the *Twowser's Down Advertiser*,' said Professor

Perfidious, fixing Dr Trotter with a steely glare. 'And that will put an end to the gossip, won't it, Twotter?' Then he paused, took a deep breath, and said, 'Now, I have a pwoposition for you.'

'Er, what's that?' said Dr Trotter.

'I would like you and your family to move to Twowser's Down,' said Professor Perfidious. 'With Dr Wedbwidge dead, sowwy, I mean *fled*, your pwesence at IFARTFASTA is more cwucial than ever. Especially as we have now come to the final phase of our gweat pwoject!' A mischievous, if not to say *murderous* glint came into his eyes as he added, 'And of course, Twotter, with your family here, there will be much, much less chance of anything, er, howwid happening to them while you are busy at work. *If* you take my meaning.'

'Er, yes, I do,' sighed Dr Trotter, miserably aware of *just* what Professor Perfidious was implying. 'But where will we live?'

'That's easy,' said Professor Perfidious. 'You can live in Cwumbling Cow Cottage, it goes with the job. After all, the pwevious occupants no longer need it. Ha ha! Not where *they've* gone…'

'No *way*!' cried Tiffany, when her mum told her about their forthcoming move. 'I can't leave Julian.

It would break my heart!' Then she stamped her foot, saying, 'You'll just have to go without me!'

'Be positive, dear,' reasoned Mrs Trotter, as optimistic as ever. 'Remember all the good things which Daddy's fantastically well-paid new job at IFARTFASTA is giving you. Like your designer jodhpurs and your lifetime subscription to *Pony* magazine. And Marbles, of course. Surely you wouldn't want to give up your beautiful, three-year-old chestnut pony?'

'Oh no…' agreed Tiffany, wavering a little.

'Exactly, dear,' said Mrs Trotter. 'We're all going to have to make sacrifices. Daddy will have to give up his membership of the local history society. Toby will have to say goodbye to all his friends at nursery. And I'm going to have to give up my dog-whispering work at Krazy K9s.' She paused before adding, quite dramatically, 'Tiffany, this move really *is* for the good of *all* of us!'

So, having finally been convinced that the wellbeing of her family should come first, Tiffany gave way and, two days later, she and Julian kissed their final 'goodbye' kiss.

'I'll text you every single day, my darling,' sobbed Tiffany. 'Do you promise to text *me*?'

'Of course,' said Julian.

Tiffany stood in the muddy lane, weeping as she gazed at the place that was to be her new home – Crumbling Cow Cottage.

'Just look at the state of it,' she sighed. 'What a dilapidated old wreck!'

'Now, now, Tiffany,' scolded Mrs Trotter. 'I know your father is slightly on the weedy side, not to mention a little bald and cross-eyed. But it's not his fault. And you must also realise that he's been under *enormous* pressure at work. Which hasn't been helped by the sudden departure of Dr Redbridge and her family.'

'I wasn't talking about Daddy,' protested Tiffany. 'I love him to pieces. I was talking about Crumbling Cow Cottage!'

But Mrs Trotter was no longer listening. She had rushed off to remind her somewhat absentminded husband that he was due to attend a *vitally* important meeting with Professor Perfidious in just one hour's time.

Tiffany wiped a stray tear from her cheek and let out a long sob of anguish. They'd only just arrived at their new home and she was already wondering if she could survive a single day apart from Julian, never mind months ... or possibly years!

'Oh, Julian,' she sighed. 'I'd gladly burn my designer jodhpurs to have you here right now.'

But he wasn't. Tiffany's gorgeous boyfriend was 80 miles away, sitting in a university hall, scribbling away at a fiendishly difficult exam paper that contained lots of long, terrifying words. Yes, in addition to being incredibly good-looking, Julian Butternut was also brainy, *breathtakingly* brainy!

And now, as if being so cruelly separated from him wasn't bad enough, Tiffany was feeling even *more* miserable. Why? Because, the very moment she'd laid eyes on Crumbling Cow Cottage, cold fingers of fear had seized her heart. As she gazed upon the ancient dwelling, with its atmosphere of foreboding and doom, instantly Tiffany had known, without a shadow of doubt, that moving to this place would turn out to be the worst decision her parents had ever made. She also knew that, sooner or later, it would bring the Trotters a whole load of trouble. What she didn't know was just how *terrible* that trouble would be ... and how soon it would all begin.

CHAPTER FOUR

Tiffany may have been feeling worried about their new home, but her ever-cheerful mum was thinking *very* differently.

'Do you know what?' she said excitedly, as they watched the removal men trying to squeeze Marbles through the doorway of their new kitchen. 'I think that life here at Trowser's Down is going to be very, very happy!'

But Mrs Trotter's words fell on deaf ears. Tiffany was lost in thoughts of her beloved Julian. Toby was playing with his toys. And Dr Trotter was just about to have his third attack of relocation rage.

'I say, you!' he cried, rushing over to the removal men and whacking the biggest one with a rolled-up copy of *Brainy Scientist Monthly*. 'Can't you see that's a pony? Look, it's got a label on it that says *stable*, so get it out of our kitchen this minute!'

'Sorry, mate,' said the removal man, who didn't appear to be all that bright. 'We thought it said table!'

'Does it *look* like a table?' snapped Dr Trotter.

'Well, it's got four legs!' protested the dim-witted oaf.

'An' a tableclof,' added his even more stupid-looking mate.

'That's its horse blanket, you twit!' shouted Dr Trotter. 'Dear me, I knew it was a mistake to use the local removals firm.' Then, instantly regretting being so rude to the two men, he calmed down for a moment and apologised for his bad manners, adding, 'By the way, how much longer are you going to be? I have a very important meeting to attend.'

'Well,' said the big one, peering at his watch. 'All being well, we should be finished when the long hand's on that thing what looks like a *tadpole*.'

'And the short one's on the, er, *stick*,' added his mate.

'Touch *wood*,' laughed the big one, giving Marbles' bottom a slap.

'They do seem a bit dozy round here, don't they, Mummy?' Tiffany whispered as her dad frantically began searching for his car keys.

Mrs Trotter blushed and glanced nervously at the two removal men, then she hid her mouth behind her hand and said, 'They say it's got something to do with the awful accident that occurred at your father's workplace.'

'What, the one that, er, never happened?' whispered Tiffany.

'Yes, that's it, dear,' Mrs Trotter whispered back. 'Apparently there was a leak of polywollysulphide gases, or bio-degenerative radioactive slime, or something. It sent one or two of the local folk sort of peculiar…'

She was interrupted by a worried-looking Dr

Trotter. 'I really must be off now, Mary!' he said, grabbing his briefcase. 'The last thing I need is to be late for my meeting with the professor.'

'Of course, dear,' said Mrs Trotter, giving her husband a quick peck on the cheek. 'I hope it goes well.'

'Yes, yes, I'm, er, sure it will,' said Dr Trotter. 'And while I'm gone, please take care, Mary. Lots and *lots* of care. And you, too, Tiffany.'

'OK, Dad,' said Tiffany. But she was only half-listening, as she was now busy texting Julian an update on the latest developments at her new home.

After watching Dr Trotter drive away, Mrs Trotter picked up Toby and went off to rescue a very confused Marbles from the removal men. Then, using her unique and remarkable talent for calming distressed dogs and other anxious animals, she soon had Marbles settled into his new stable, snorting contentedly and doing all the other things that happy horses do.

Tiffany quickly read through her text:

Darling Sherbet Fountain, have just arrived at Crumbling Cow Cottage. It's a wreck and people here are

weird! I'm afraid something bad will
happen soon. Miss you loads. How did
the exam go? Love always, Fizzy Pips
XXX

Then, happy with what she'd written, she pressed 'send' and instantly felt happier. In just a few moments, her gorgeous boyfriend would be replying with reassuring words that were guaranteed to make her feel a whole lot better. Her heart fluttering with anticipation, Tiffany waited for the familiar *kerchung-ping-twattle-twattle-ping*! sound that would tell her Julian's text had arrived.

But nothing came. Which was odd, because Julian was normally incredibly quick to reply to text messages.

Another minute passed. Then another minute. And still no reply! Just when she was beginning to despair, *kerchung-ping-twattle-twattle-ping*! went her phone, and her heart leapt with joy. Eagerly, she scanned Julian's message:

Hi Alex, it was great to meet you
today. Perhaps we can get together
some time and continue our chat? Fancy
grabbing a coffee after the next exam?

Julian Butternut (the tall, handsome
one who picked up your pen)

Tiffany read the message again and her blood ran cold. Surely not! Surely her beloved couldn't be thinking of getting together with some girl called Alex. Not *her* Julian. He'd sworn he'd never love another. Ever! But then Tiffany remembered that Alex was also a boy's name and she breathed a sigh of relief. It was all just a silly misunderstanding. Surely. Nevertheless, a whole load of doubts now began niggling at her mind.

CHAPTER FIVE

At around the same time that Tiffany was worrying about Julian's text, Dr Trotter was sitting outside Professor Perfidious's office, fiddling frantically with a securely stoppered test tube in which hundreds of pale-pink tadpole things wiggled and burped. As he fiddled, he thought back to the time he had first noticed the strange changes happening to his employer.

It was when he and Dr Redbridge had chanced upon some quite astonishing discoveries. Not only had these findings set Professor Perfidious's mind on a new and extremely *dangerous* train of thought, they'd also revealed aspects of his personality that the two scientists found very disturbing.

Dr Trotter recalled how Professor Perfidious had acted when they'd shown him what they'd found out.

'Oh, Dr Twotter, Dr Wedbwidge, these unforeseen wesults of yours have set my mind wacing!' he'd said, dancing wildly around the laboratory, his eyes glittering with excitement. 'The possibilities are endless! It's what I've been pwaying for!'

'You're right there,' said Dr Redbridge. 'Our magnificent laboratories and top-of-the-range equipment must have cost you a fortune!'

'No, not *paying*, you fool!' yelled Professor Perfidious. '*Pwaying*!' You know, going down on my knees and stuff.' Then his eyes narrowed as he hissed, 'Yesss, secwetly pwaying for this once-in-a-lifetime opportunity for *wevenge, wetwibution* and *wepwisal*!'

Not long after that, urged on by an increasingly mad professor, who had forgotten all about their original project, Dr Trotter and Dr Redbridge had become involved in a set of completely new and very risky experiments. Experiments that were already producing some incredibly scary results!

'Urrgh! They're so *wevolting*, but so *magnificent*,' Professor Perfidious had drooled one stormy afternoon, as the three of them peered at the grotesque 'products' of the day's work. 'Now, we must wefine and wemodel these cweatures, giving them extwaordinawy powers beyond those of any other living being. We must make them wesilient to whatever can be thwown at them, be it bombs, bullets or bwicks. And, finally, we must twain them to obey our evewy command!'

'But what about the *rightness* of what we are doing?' protested Dr Redbridge.

'Or some might say, the *wrongness*,' added Dr Trotter, equally ill at ease.

'*Wightness*!' exploded Perfidious, as lightning zig-zagged across Trowser's Down and bathed him in an eerie blue glow. '*Wongness*! It is quite plain to me that you, Dr Twotter, never had your head pushed down the toilet when you were at pwep school. Not just once, but evewy single day. And no doubt you, Dr Wedbwidge, have never known the sowwow of being weferred to by the other bwats as Jewemy the Giwaffe!'

The two scientists shook their heads and agreed they hadn't.

And then, as the thunder rumbled across the slopes of Trowser's Down and lightning sparked around IFARTFASTA's satellite dishes and radio masts, Professor Perfidious began striding up and down the laboratory, slapping wildly at imaginary 'bwats'.

'All my life, I have been cwuelly widiculed!' he ranted. 'Never once having a twue fwend. And now fate has pwesented me with this bwilliant opportunity to put a lifetime's wongs wight. I've had a long time to wait but, finally, I *will* have my wevenge!' Then, blushing slightly, he added, 'And, never having had the good fortune to enjoy a womantic welationship, I think it would also be very nice for me to finally have a family of my

32

own, don't you?' He glared at the two scientists, his piercing green eyes seeming to slice through their very souls. 'And one more thing,' Professor Perfidious had said. 'We must have no more *wunaways*! Please wemember to double-check the locks on the birthing pools and twansmutation chambers when you leave. You will no doubt be delighted to learn that I have wecently pwovided my securwity staff with a twio of fierce Wottweillers and ordered them to be extwa vigilant!'

Then, with a dramatic flourish of his cape, he'd left the laboratory, leaving the two scientists open-mouthed with shock and terror.

'TWOTTER! TWOTTER! WAKE UP! STOP DAYDWEAMING, MAN! WE'VE WORK TO GET ON WITH!'

Dr Trotter looked up to see Professor Perfidious towering over him. Rather than his usual cape, moleskin trousers and polo neck, the professor was dressed in a bizarre brown uniform. From its various loops and flaps there dangled dozens of military decorations and medals. All of which, on closer examination, proved to be nothing more than an assortment of shiny bottle tops and bits of cheap coloured ribbon. In one hand he held a very mean-looking whip, and in the other an enormous six-shooter, which he twirled menacingly, like a desperado in a Wild West movie.

'Professor Perfidious!' said Dr Trotter. 'I'm sorry. I was lost in thought.'

'Well, that's as may be, Twotter!' barked Professor Perfidious. 'But now it's time for us to be vewy, vewy busy. The gweat day has finally awwived. Come, let us pwoceed to the Alpha Birthing Pool. Our wemarkable cweations await us. We are about to make histowy, Twotter. Histowy!'

CHAPTER SIX

Tiffany sighed and smiled. All was now clear. Just a few minutes ago, a second text had arrived from Julian. She read it for the third time, her heart bursting with love for him again:

> Darling Fizzy Pips, sorry about the last text. I'm so miserable about leaving you, I sent the wrong one. Alex is a guy I met this morning. Don't worry too much about your new house being horrid and the locals being weird. Moving house is one of the most stressful things you can do - you'll feel better about everything soon. BTW exam a piece of cake. Yours for ever, Sherbert Fountain XXX

Tiffany was just about to read the text a fourth time when she was interrupted by her mum.

'Listen, Tiffany!' Mrs Trotter said cheerfully. 'The removal men are nearly done. As soon as they're gone, I'm going to pop Toby in his trailer and then cycle over to Trowser's Down village to buy something for dinner. While I'm out, why don't you go for a ride? Marbles will be glad of the exercise after being cooped up all day.'

'All right,' said Tiffany, remembering how she'd promised herself that, no matter how miserable she felt, she would still make sure she looked after her precious Marbles.

'It's such a lovely afternoon,' her mum said encouragingly. 'You could take a picnic and make the most of the sunshine. With luck, you might even bump into some girls from the local pony club!'

So, ten minutes later, Tiffany led Marbles from his stable and saddled him up.

'Have a good time, dear,' said Mrs Trotter. 'And make sure you take care when you're up on Trowser's Down. The removal men have just been telling me some very silly stories about the place.'

'Like what?' said Tiffany.

'Well,' said Mrs Trotter. 'They say that recently some rather odd-looking things have been spotted wandering around.'

'What do you mean *odd-looking things*?' said Tiffany.

'Well, I suppose what they're talking about are *creatures*,' said Mrs Trotter. 'Apparently they're neither one thing nor another!'

'What, mutants or something?' said Tiffany, slightly taken aback.

'Yes, I *guess* that's what they mean,' said Mrs Trotter. 'The locals call them Hodgepodges. Apparently some are very, *very* freakish indeed. You know, like huge chickens with the heads of rabbits!'

'Yuk!' said Tiffany, truly appalled.

'Yes, yuk!' her mum agreed. Then she paused, before adding, 'But they do seem to be a very primitive and ignorant lot round here, don't they, so I wouldn't worry too much. It's probably all just a load of gossip.'

'Of course,' laughed Tiffany. 'I'm sure there's absolutely nothing to be frightened of!'

CHAPTER SEVEN

Dr Trotter had never felt so afraid. He knew that in the next hour, he would be doing things that would change the world. And not in a good way, but in a *terrible* way. He also knew that, once he'd done those awful things, there'd be no going back. *Ever.* This was his very last chance to change his mind. He took a deep breath. It was now or never…

'Yes,' he thought. 'Just like my tragic and sorely missed colleague, Dr Pamela Redbridge, I will finally stand up to the foul professor and refuse to give in to any more of his outrageous demands. And in that way I will save mankind from the terrible devastation he is about to wreak on so many innocent people!'

But then Dr Trotter remembered all those blood-curdling screams and angry yells of, 'Perfidious, Perfidious! That's what you are, Perfidious!' that he'd heard coming from the Transmutation Chamber at IFARTFASTA the day after the Redbridges had disappeared. The screams and yells that had been followed by the revolting *crunch-crunch-crunch* of human bones and the stench of sizzling flesh. Then, finally ... silence!

Dr Trotter shuddered. The thought of anything like that happening to his own family made his blood run cold, and in that instant he was aware that he would do *whatever* Professor Perfidious asked of him. *Whatever* the consequences.

Professor Perfidious had a list. It contained the names and addresses of all the people who had ever upset him. Like the woman who'd failed to thank him when he'd held a door open for her back in 1983. The people who'd laughed so 'cwuelly' when he'd fallen down the escalator in a department store. The roomful of *other* professors who'd *failed* to laugh when he told them the joke about the hedgehog and the laboratory assistant. Then there were all the children and teachers from his schooldays. And so it went on…

Furthermore, the professor was now feeling especially hard done by. His demand that Dr Trotter and Dr Redbridge 'cweate' the family he yearned for had failed. Unfortunately, the DNA they'd taken from his fingernails to kick-start the process hadn't been quite up to scratch.

To put it mildly, the children he'd so longed for hadn't quite turned out as he'd hoped. And, having failed to bond with a couple of them when they'd gone completely bananas during a game of snakes and ladders, a bruised and confused Professor Perfidious had ordered they be 'put back in their storwage vats until they learn pwoper manners!'

But then this pair of bizarre and temperamental, not to mention *extremely dangerous*, experiments-gone-wrong had unexpectedly vanished overnight.

Dr Trotter had put this down to them simply melting away, due to things like tissue rejection, incompatible internal organs and the complete breakdown of their cell structures. However, having later found two sets of wet footprints leading out of the storage area, he had begun to suspect otherwise.

'Good widdance to the little bwats, I say!' the professor had snarled. And no more was said on the matter.

But all this meant that Professor Perfidious's plans were rapidly moving beyond mere revenge. A new idea was forming in his mind. If the world didn't suit him, why couldn't he change it so it did? He had the means of doing so, and the idea was becoming more and more appealing.

'Well,' thought Dr Trotter, as he followed the professor down the spiral staircase that led to the Alpha Birthing Pool. 'If anything goes wrong, at least I can be sure my loved ones are safe in Crumbling Cow Cottage. Heaven knows what might happen to them if they were out on Trowser's Down. Once these devilish creatures are loose they'll –' But then he stopped himself, not wanting to think about the monstrosities he was about to unleash on an unsuspecting world.

CHAPTER EIGHT

As Marbles galloped across Trowser's Down, the wind in his mane and his ordeal with the removal men entirely forgotten, Tiffany could see her pony was truly happy. However, the same could not be said about herself. Despite the pleasant warmth of the sun on her skin, Tiffany's heart still ached at being so cruelly separated from her beloved Julian. And now, in addition to that, all sorts of worrying questions had begun to nag furiously at her brain. Like what had *really* happened to the Redbridges? And were those rumours of odd-looking creatures being loose on Trowser's Down true?

Making a big effort to push all thoughts of freaky folk from her mind, Tiffany clicked her tongue, and with a cry of, 'Come on, Marbles old boy!' she urged her pony on.

This is more like it, she thought, as Marbles jumped streams and raced past old stone barns. But as they began to climb the steep heather-covered slope which led to Trowser's Down itself, her mood became dark and troubled once again. This may have been because her mind was suddenly plagued with a whole new set of worries about Julian's text to 'Alex'. Or it may have been because a swirling mist was beginning to fall across the Down, rapidly blocking out the bright afternoon sunlight. But it was most likely due to the fact that she suddenly had the strange feeling she was being watched. And now, casting an anxious glance behind her, she saw that not only was she being watched, she was also being *followed*!

'Twotter!' oozed Professor Perfidious, as they surveyed the huge tank of bubbling green slime, which was the Alpha Birthing Pool. 'You weally have excelled yourself this time!'

Just beneath the surface of the churning ooze, it was possible to see shapes moving about. But, just as it's impossible to make out the details of fish swimming in a murky pond, it was also extremely difficult to see the details of these things. However, every now and then, a slime-covered head would break the surface, or a strangely contorted claw would reach up and grab frantically at thin air.

'How long before they are weddy?' Professor

Perfidious asked excitedly, peering into the depths.

'Well, Professor,' said Dr Trotter. 'As I said before, I could have done with a few more weeks to fine-tune their indestructibility genes and –'

'Yes, yes, I *know* all that,' Professor Perfidious interrupted. 'But as *I* said, *I* can't wait a moment longer. So, how long, Twotter?'

'About another twenty minutes,' sighed Dr Trotter. 'All I have to do now is to administer methelone-T zygotes and the tetremetacyclotropin HB3, and then we can begin the final fusing.'

'Good, good!' hissed Professor Perfidious, pointing to the video cameras that had been set up around the room. 'I will be wecording evewy moment of this histowic occasion! Oh, it is all so thwilling! Especially as neither of us are *entirely* sure what will finally emerge from that wepugnant soup. No doubt when the cweatures begin to show themselves, we will have a few surpwises. I love surpwises, don't you, Twotter?'

'Absolutely,' replied Dr Trotter, though he didn't sound too sure.

'Yes, yes!' hissed Professor Perfidious. Then his gaunt features turned as cold as stone as he added, 'By the way, Twotter, if you have any ideas about twying to *sabotage* my gweat pwoject, I should think again. At this moment, Zoltan, Cholera and Pancreas, my twio of twustworthy secuwity men and their fewocious and highly twained Wottweillers are on their way to Cwumbling Cow Cottage. All it will take is one pwess of a button and they will weceive a text orderwing them to do exactly as I have instwucted. You do love your family, don't you, Twotter?'

'Of course I do,' said Dr Trotter. 'I've no intention of letting you down, Professor!'

And now, abandoning all hope of ruining the

professor's evil scheme, Dr Trotter took a deep breath, unscrewed the stopper from the test tube, prayed for a miracle, and tipped its contents into the Alpha Birthing Pool.

CHAPTER NINE

Tiffany's heart pounded. She was being stalked! Some hideously misshapen *thing* was moving along the edge of Trowser's Down, following her every movement. However, because of the gathering mist, it was hard to make out this *thing* in detail. What she *could* see was whoever or *whatever* the thing appeared to be, it was taking a very close interest in her.

All at once, the words 'creatures' and 'neither one thing nor another' came into Tiffany's mind and she went weak at the elbows. Could this be one of the Hodgepodges that were causing so much alarm? And, if so, was she in danger?

As if in answer to her questions, the creature began scrambling down the hillside, heading straight for her. Tiffany now spotted something glinting in the last ray of sunshine. She clapped a hand to her mouth then let out a brief whimper of anxiety. The *thing* was carrying some sort of long, dangerous-looking object like an enormous knife or spear, but it was hard to tell.

Oh, if *only* Julian was here, Tiffany thought. He'd know what to do. Which reminded her — she hadn't texted him for ages. She took out her mobile and dashed off what might be her last ever message:

> Darling Sherbert Fountain, on Trowser's
> Down being stalked by horrible mutant
> thing. Am completely terrified! Hope
> it doesn't do anything horrid to me.
> Love always, Fizzy Pips XXX

The creature was now just 200 metres away. Tiffany was so captivated by its looming presence, she didn't notice when Julian failed to reply. All her thoughts were taken up with the *thing*. It was clear there was something very peculiar about it. However, the mist was so thick and Tiffany was so terrified, she couldn't quite put her finger on what it was.

It may have been the fact that the creature's skull was hideously deformed with a huge jutting forehead, which sort of dangled over its eyes. Or that it had a gruesome, carrot-shaped growth poking up from its neck. Or that an enormous camel-like hump bulged from its back and wobbled quite sickeningly as it moved. Or it may have been that it appeared to be dressed in the sort of checked flared trousers, diamond-patterned tank top and two-tone shoes that had gone out of fashion some time before the First Ice Age. And now the thing was beginning to run her way, waving wildly and pointing at something behind her.

'Well, matey, you've got another thing coming,' she thought. 'As if I'm going to fall for the old look-out-there's-something-behind-you trick. Get real, pudding face!'

Tiffany was now faced with a terrible dilemma. Should she simply sit and wait for the *thing* to reach her, then attempt to involve it in pleasant conversation about how best to limit one's carbon footprint? Or should she simply engage it in ferocious hand-to-hand combat, using her teeth, elbows and nails to pluck out its eyes and smash its bones? After all, she had once spent a summer holiday at a young ladies' survival school, where she and lots of other girls had been taught how to live off geraniums for a week and beat an 18-stone mugger to a pulp.

She decided to go for the eye-plucking and bone-smashing. Well, the course had cost her mum and dad a fortune. They'd be pleased to know they'd got their money's worth.

Leaping from Marble's back, Tiffany went into a menacing crouch, snarling savagely, her lips curled back and her fingers assuming the martial arts 'angry bushbaby' stance she'd been taught. Next, for dramatic effect, she spun round a few times, which wasn't a good idea, because suddenly feeling incredibly sick and dizzy, she fell over, and by the time she got back to her feet, the thing had vanished.

The creature now had her at a distinct disadvantage. There was only one thing for it – she would infuriate it with a series of insults, in the hope that it would burst from its cover and launch an angry attack on her, which she could instantly counter with a dazzling display of martial arts.

Feet apart, head cocked in a gesture of devil-may-care defiance, Tiffany put her hands on her hips and let loose a stream of brutal verbs, nouns and adjectives that surprised even her.

'COME ON THEN, YOU LILY-LIVERED WIMP!' she heard herself snarl. 'I'M GONNA TEAR OFF YOUR LEGS AND RIP OFF YOUR EARS! AND THAT'S JUST FOR STARTERS!'

She paused, trying to think of something else to say. But as she did, she saw a flash of movement from the corner of her eye. She turned, fully expecting to see the *thing* charging at her. But it wasn't. It was Marbles. And, rather than charging at her, her pony was running away.

Suddenly, all Tiffany's thoughts of taking on the creature were replaced by complete panic.

'Marbles, wait for me!' she yelled. 'It wasn't *your* legs I was talking about. Please come back, Marbles. I love you!'

She began to chase after her pony. However, she had barely taken three steps when she felt her arms being firmly grasped by two sets of very large fleshy hands, and she heard a voice say, 'Hello! Will you be our *fwend*?'

CHAPTER TEN

'Oh, fiddlesticks,' said Mrs Trotter, recognising the telltale hiss of escaping air. 'What a time to have a puncture. And here's me thinking how clever I was to have taken the short cut to the village by cycling over Trowser's Down. Now we're stuck in the middle of nowhere! Oh dear, Toby, what *are* we going to do?'

Then she spotted a dark smudge on the horizon. And, as the smudge drew nearer, she thought, 'Well, that is a stroke of luck. I didn't expect to see another vehicle up here!'

Admittedly, the vehicle was being driven in a rather erratic manner, swerving wildly from one side of the road to the other. And there did appear to be some sort of chaotic event taking place inside it, involving lots of barking, shouting and terrified screaming.

But, as Mrs Trotter said to Toby as she stepped into the middle of the road, 'Ah well, any port in a storm!' And she began to flag down the very rusty old black van.

'What a strange afternoon I'm having,' thought Tiffany. 'First I'm stalked by that horrid, camel-humped Hodgepodge creature. Then my Marbles disappears. And now I bump into *this* pair of oddballs!'

For a moment, she wondered if she really *had* lost her marbles, or if she was dreaming. But the strong fleshy fingers that pressed so painfully into her arms told her she wasn't.

Tiffany had never seen such a monstrous-looking pair of children. They had round smiley faces and big innocent eyes. They were also very dribbly, very snotty and very, very smelly. Both of them must have been at least six-foot tall. And as for fat. Well, she'd heard of childhood obesity, but this was ridiculous. They each must have weighed 12 stone, *minimum*. And, just to make their appearance even *more* peculiar, they were wearing white Wellington boots, science-lab safety goggles and bright-yellow plastic waste sacks with holes cut out for their big pink heads.

Tiffany quickly decided that had she met this pair of hideous freaks under any other circumstances, she most certainly would have crossed the road to avoid them. But, given that they were firmly gripping her arms in their vice-like fingers, she didn't really have that option right now.

'Will you, will you ... will you be our *fwend*?' gurgled the giant girl.

'Yes, will you?' drooled the giant boy. 'It would make us both *vewy* happy!'

Trying hard to ignore the enormous cluster of gooey green bogies that the boy had just wiped on her sleeve, Tiffany cried, 'Of course I'll be your friend. In fact, I wanted to be your friend the moment I saw you. You're both just so gorgeous!'

'Are we?' cried the boy, splashing Tiffany with warm spit and looking quite delighted.

'That's not what Daddy told us,' said the girl. 'He said we were bwats!'

'So we wan away,' added the boy.

'Well,' said Tiffany, mentally sifting through a selection of possible escape plans. 'If we're going to be friends, we'd better introduce ourselves. My name's Tiffany. 'What are you called?'

'I'm Woseanne,' said the girl. 'And he's –'

'Wobert,' said the boy. 'Wobert Pewegwine Perfidious.'

CHAPTER ELEVEN

One by one, Dr Trotter's 'creations' began to emerge from the Alpha Birthing Pool. And, just as he was deciding that the one appearing now couldn't *possibly* be as freakish or fearsome as the last, it turned out to be even more so. In the scientist's worst nightmares, he could never have imagined such a gruesome assortment of misshapen monstrosities. Next to these creatures, the most hideous horror-film creations would look sweet and cuddly.

Some had warty heads, swollen to the size of beach balls, perched precariously on tiny torsos. Others had puny, withered skulls that sat on vulture-like necks attached to gargantuan bodies. Some had staring yellow eyes, stumpy noses and flappy ears. Others resembled horribly deformed, walking vegetables. From the faces of some, scarlet-veined eyes stared out, while huge crimson, dribbling mouths opened to reveal row after row of rotting, yellow fangs. But all of his 'creations' had one thing in common. Each and every one of them gave off an overwhelming feeling of unlimited power and ruthless savagery…

Soon, about fifty creatures had climbed out of the pool and were clustered at its edge, shuffling, blinking and murmuring as horrid, yellowish-pink slime dripped from their newborn bodies. Occasionally, one would move away from the others, then throw back its head and let out a long blood-curdling howl. After which it would quietly return to the murmuring shuffling throng, having satisfied itself that it was now fully alive.

'This is the first batch, Professor,' said Dr Trotter. 'Do you wish me to begin birthing the next cluster?'

'No! No!' cried Professor Perfidious. 'For the time being, these will do nicely.' Then he stepped back and let out a long, satisfied sigh. 'They weally are wemarkable, Twotter,' he whispered, as his companion shuddered with revulsion. 'You have done us pwoud!'

'Thank you,' mumbled Dr Trotter, almost choking on his words.

'Now,' gushed the professor, hopping excitedly from one foot to the other. 'We must get them pwoperly clothed. After all, it wouldn't be wight to let them loose on my enemies in such a state of undwess.'

He clapped his hands and with a cry of, 'Chop chop! We haven't a moment to waste!' began directing his creations through a door marked Dressing Room.

The creatures shuffled inside and began rummaging amongst piles of clothing, seemingly programmed to obey his every command. After several minutes they re-emerged, now dressed in such a bizarre and ill-assorted collection of outfits that, if the situation hadn't been so deadly serious, Dr Trotter would have laughed out loud.

Suddenly looking ill at ease, Professor Perfidious blushed and said, 'Yes, I *know* what you're thinking, Twotter! Their, er, clothes aren't *quite* what I had in mind. I was hoping for something wather more *wegimental.*' He gestured to his own uniform. 'However, even my funds have limits. And you must admit, it weally is wemarkable what one can pick up in chawity shops.'

'Yes, er, remarkable,' said Dr Trotter, pretending to admire one horse-faced specimen clad in a pink sequinned dress that had obviously once belonged to a *very* small woman.

Others had kitted themselves out in pastel-coloured tracksuits that even the dead wouldn't be seen dead in. Some wore school uniforms several sizes too small for them, which they'd combined with a fantastic assortment of scarves, bowler hats, sombreros and berets. Others had on flowery Bermuda shorts teamed with skimpy halter-neck tops. One particularly repulsive and extremely blotchy creature had kitted itself out in a very small bikini.

Professor Perfidious now began to herd his creations up the spiral staircase and into the conference room of IFARTFASTA, where he planned to give them their welcome speech. Soon, he had them standing in lines, still shuffling, murmuring and grunting, but surprisingly well behaved for such a terrifying collection of misfits and monsters.

Looking for all the world like the power-crazed freak he had now become, Professor Perfidious climbed onto a small stage and raised his hands for silence. Immediately, a hush fell over the creatures.

'Gweetings, loyal subjects!' cried the professor.

'Gweetings to you, oh exalted one!' the freaks roared back.

'Thank you! Thank you!' cried the professor. 'I'm so pleased to see you all looking so fabulous in your new outfits. But now to business, my subjects. I have bwought you here today for a very special weason.'

'Please tell us about it, oh glorwious one!' roared the freaks.

'I will!' yelled Professor Perfidious. 'It is like this. Over the years, many howwid individuals have dared to diswespect me!'

'Never!' roared the freaks. 'We don't believe it!'

'Yes, they did,' continued Professor Perfidious. 'And in doing so, they have made me vewy, vewy angwy!'

Praying that the floor might suddenly open up and swallow him on the spot, Dr Trotter watched the professor remove a thick bundle of papers from his tunic then wave it in front of him, yelling, 'All their names and addwesses are wight here! And you, my fwends have a vewy special task to perform. In just a short time, you will go forth and weak havoc amongst these people!'

'Sounds like *fun!*' roared the freaks.

'It will be!' yelled the professor. 'And please feel fwee to do whatever you like. No punishment is too cwuel or tewwible for these wetches. Stwangle them, mangle them and fangle them. They have only themselves to blame. Do you understand, my childwen?'

'We understand, oh wonderful one!' roared the freaks.

'Splendid, splendid!' cried the professor. 'Now, some of you may be wondewing about your safety. Once you're loose in the community, spweading tewwor and dwead, the authowities will, of course, twy to stop you. But do not fear, I have made each and evewy one of you indestwuctible!'

At this point, Dr Trotter began tugging urgently at Professor Perfidious's sleeve and whispering, 'But they *aren't* indestructible, Professor. I told you they weren't. You didn't give me time to finish that bit…'

'Oh, fiddlesticks, Twotter!' Professor Perfidious hissed angrily, roughly elbowing the scientist aside and yelling, 'YES, MY FWENDS, YOU ARE TOTALLY IN-DEST-WUCT-IBLE!'

'Thwee cheers for our Supweme Maker!' screamed the freaks. Then they began jumping up and down and applauding wildly.

'Yes, it's twue!' shouted Professor Perfidious, raising his hands for calm. 'Neither bwicks, battle-axes, bombs or booby twaps can harm you!'

The freaks cheered again. But this time the applause was interrupted by a particularly powerful-looking specimen, who raised its hand and said, 'Er, please may I ask a question?'

'Of course you can,' said Professor Perfidious.

'Well,' said the creature. 'When you went thwough that list of stuff that wouldn't harm us, you didn't mention bullets.'

'Ha!' laughed Professor Perfidious. 'Don't worry. Bullets are one of the things against which you are *most* indestwuctible!'

And now, as Dr Trotter covered his face with his hands, the professor went on, 'If any of you doubt my words, I will pwove the twuth of that statement. But first I need a volunteer.'

The freaks all suddenly took a keen interest in their feet.

'All wight, I will *choose* a volunteer,' said Professor Perfidious, and he pointed to the creature who had asked the question. 'You, since you're the one who wants to know. What's your name?'

'Howace,' said the creature.

'Well, Howace, come here.'

The creature did as it was told. A moment later, it was standing directly in front of Professor Perfidious.

'Now, Howace,' he said reassuringly. 'I give you my word, you are in no danger. Are you all wight with that?'

Horace nodded.

'Stand vewy, vewy still,' said Professor Perfidious, raising his pistol and pointing it at Horace's massive, bucket-shaped head. 'I pwomise this will not hurt.'

Horror stricken, Dr Trotter peeped out between his fingers, just in time to see the professor release the pistol's safety catch, pull the trigger … and fire.

An instant later, Horace's head exploded like a pumpkin that had just been hit with a sledgehammer, showering Professor Perfidious and Dr Trotter with blood, brain and bone.

CHAPTER TWELVE

At the mention of the name Perfidious, Tiffany's mind began to whirl and her legs turned to jelly. Nevertheless, she realised that if she were going to survive this awful situation, she would need to remain calm.

So she took a deep breath and said, 'Well, Roseanne and Robert, if we're going to be friends, do you think you could let go of my arms? It's starting to hurt.'

'Of course we can!' the huge children cried, and immediately released Tiffany's arms, only to seize hold of her hands, gripping them just as tightly and still making escape impossible.

'Tiffany,' said Robert. 'Have you got good taste?'

'Er, I think so,' said Tiffany, slightly surprised by the question. 'I always choose my clothes very carefully.'

'No, Wobert doesn't mean *that*,' said Roseanne.

67

'He means do you taste *nice*?'

'Yes,' said Robert. 'You see, Tiffany, we've been following you for a long time. And earlier on we had a wow.'

'A wow?' said Tiffany.

'Yes, a wow,' said Robert. 'We couldn't decide whether to eat you stwaight away. Or be your fwend first.'

'So we thought we'd do both.'

'And now we've been your fwend, it's time to eat you!'

'You *are* joking, aren't you?' said Tiffany.

'No,' said Roseanne. 'We're vewy, vewy hungwy. We've been wandering around for days. And all we've had to eat is gweat big chickens with heads like wabbits.'

'And gweat big wabbits with heads like chickens,' added Robert. 'So *you* should make a nice change.'

'Baggsy me first bite!' squealed Roseanne.

'Hmmm, yummy yummy, yum yum,' drooled Robert.

Tiffany braced herself, wondering which part of her anatomy Roseanne would sink her teeth into first when she heard the familiar *kerchung-ping-twattle-twattle-ping*! of her mobile phone.

'A text message!' she gasped, suddenly

remembering that she was expecting a reply from Julian and, despite her situation, she cheered up at once. 'Would you mind if I just read it before you get stuck in? It might, you know, help me cope with, er, you know, being *eaten*!'

'Feel fwee,' said Roseanne.

'No pwobs,' added Robert.

Tiffany clicked on the message. Sure enough, it was from Julian. But then, as she began to read, her already-broken heart began to self-destruct...

Tiffany, your increasingly hysterical texts are becoming a real pain. Please stop sending such nonsense and consider seeking help at once. Sorry, but I think we should end things between us. Not only because of your strange behaviour, but also because I have just met an amazing girl called Alex. Next to her you would be improved by a paper bag on your head. Not yours anymore, Julian

Tiffany couldn't believe it. All her doubts about her boyfriend had been right – Julian *had* met someone new! Unable to bear thinking about it, she began to sob and shake like she had never done before.

'Oh dear,' gasped Roseanne, truly shocked by the uncontrollably quivering, blubbering Tiffany. 'What's the matter? Shall I wait a few more minutes before ... tucking in?'

'No, please – go ahead,' sobbed Tiffany. 'What's a few minutes of a life that is now utterly, *utterly* worthless.' Then, really getting into her stride, she seized one of Roseanne's massive arms and screamed, 'In fact, now I actually *want* you to eat me. Go on – tuck in, you great fat slob. Chew my face off. According to Mr Smarty Pants here, apparently it's *hideous!*'

'Oh, all right then, if you insist,' said Roseanne, and she rammed a substantial area of Tiffany's face into her gigantic, dribbly mouth.

However, before she could actually sink in her teeth, there was a sudden, loud *thwack!* and something hit Roseanne on the ear.

'Ouch!' she yelled, instantly releasing her hold on Tiffany. 'What was that?'

'Ha ha!' cried Robert. 'That was funny, Woseanne. You should have seen yourself jump!'

At which point, there was another loud *thwack!* and something hit Robert on the ear. A moment later, a golf ball landed at Tiffany's feet.

More *thwacks*! followed, each accompanied by cries of pain from Robert and Roseanne. Tiffany looked up to see that the air was now filled with flying golf balls, all clouting and clobbering the enormous infants. But, amazingly, not a single one was hitting *her*!

It was all too much for the huge children. Covering their heads with their hands and howling in pain, they fell to their knees and made a desperate attempt to crawl away. But still the onslaught continued and, just seconds later, Robert collapsed in a groaning heap, shortly followed by Roseanne. After a few few moments, the awful infants went very, very still, their enormous bodies now completely lifeless.

Tiffany let out a long sigh, realising she had just had a very narrow escape. She also realised that, despite the awful message from Julian, she still very much wanted to remain alive.

Her relief was short-lived. Tiffany now saw a familiar figure coming towards her, and her heart sank. It was the camel-humped Hodgepodge that had been stalking her twenty minutes ago. And now it was leading a pony. The Hodgepodge had captured her Marbles!

'Here we go again,' Tiffany groaned. 'Out of the frying pan, into the fire…'

However, the mist was now beginning to clear and, as it did, Tiffany realised that the thing wasn't quite as menacing as she'd first thought. Now she could plainly see that what she'd taken to be a horribly deformed forehead was actually the peak of a golfer's cap. While the carrot-shaped growth sprouting from its neck was, in reality, a large tuft of blond hair, which poked from the back of that same cap. And the gruesome hump on its back was actually a very large golf bag. Furthermore, what she had taken to be a lethal weapon, was actually nothing more than a golf club!

In fact, she could now clearly see that the Hodgepodge wasn't a Hodgepodge at all, but a teenage boy dressed in golfing clothes. And a very good-looking teenage boy at that, who was now standing in front of her holding her pony, a winning smile spread across his handsome face.

'That was a close thing,' he grinned, giving Marbles an affectionate pat as he handed Tiffany the reins. 'I thought those two had you for sure. They've been following you for ages. I tried to warn you earlier, but you obviously thought I was some sort of threat, too. However, all that martial arts stuff you did was very impressive. Well … until you fell over!' He laughed and Tiffany blushed. Ignoring her embarrassment, the boy continued, 'Oh dear, I'm forgetting my manners. I haven't introduced myself. My name's Nigel, Nigel Redbridge.'

CHAPTER THIRTEEN

As Horace's body slumped to the floor, the monsters let out a great gasp of shock. Some of them even buried their faces in their hands and groaned in disbelief.

'Oh dear,' said Professor Perfidious. 'That wasn't supposed to happen, was it, Twotter?'

'Er, no, it wasn't,' said Dr Trotter, wiping a crimson splash from his cheek. 'But I did warn you that we were rushing the indestructibility side of things. It really could have done with another few more weeks' work.'

The twitching corpse lay at Professor Perfidious's feet, blood still spurting from the ragged stump where his head had once been. As they gazed down at it, Dr Trotter and Professor Perfidious became aware of the sound of angry murmuring coming from amongst the freaks.

'Oh no!' yelled an angry voice. 'He's murdered Howace!'

'Er, any chance of making him better, Twotter?' whispered a panic-stricken professor, nodding anxiously at the now-stiffening body. 'You know, a sort of quick fix. Just to restore their confidence in me.'

'Sorry,' said Dr Trotter, shaking his head. 'Even I couldn't do that.'

The murmuring had now increased to a mutinous roar and the horse-faced monstrosity in the pink mini-dress was shaking its fist at Professor Perfidious, yelling, 'Howace twusted you. And you killed him!'

'Yes, you betwayed him!' yelled one of the creatures.

'Perhaps he's planning to kill us all!' called horse-face.

'Let's get him before he gets us!' cried another monster.

All at once, the entire mass began surging towards the platform, yelling, 'Yes! Yes! Kill Lofty! Kill the gweat, bird-faced beanpole!'

'Stop that this minute,' said Professor Perfidious, pointing his pistol at the advancing horde. 'Stop, or I'll fire!'

'You'll only get a few of us!' yelled horse-face. 'The west will tear you to pieces!' Then, before

Professor Perfidious could fire a shot, the massive creature leapt onto the platform, knocked the professor to the floor and seized him by the throat.

'So,' said Nigel, as he and Tiffany started to walk home. 'Professor Perfidious was very angry with my mum for refusing to help in his crazy cloning scheme. Not long after they had their row, Zoltan, Cholera and Pancreas turned up at our house and took us all to IFARTFASTA. When we got there, the professor made one last attempt to try and persuade Mum to carry on with the work by telling her all the horrible things that would happen to us if she refused. But Mum's conviction about doing the right thing was far more important to us than getting hurt. We didn't care what they did, as long as Mum stuck by her principles!'

'Unlike my dad?' said Tiffany, suddenly feeling rather uncomfortable.

'Don't worry, it wasn't quite like that,' said Nigel. 'Let me explain what happened next, and then perhaps you'll understand –'

But, before he could finish, Nigel was interrupted by the rumble of an engine and the two of them looked up to see a very rusty old black van bouncing and bumping towards them. A moment later, it came to a halt, its back doors opened and three huge Rottweillers jumped out, closely followed by Zoltan, Cholera and Pancreas.

Dr Trotter's time had arrived. Without a moment's hesitation, he ripped off his white lab coat and specs. These were quickly followed by his bow tie, shirt, shoes and trousers. Now, revealed in all his fabulous glory, the all-new, anatomically enhanced scientist leapt at the horse-faced creature that was doing its best to throttle Professor Perfidious.

With his massive pecs swelling, his enormous deltoids throbbing and his superbly developed biceps twitching, Dr Trotter dragged the creature off the professor as easily as he would have pulled a kitten off a mouse. Then, as if the murderous monster weighed no more than a feather, he raised him high above his head, rushed at the mob of advancing freaks, and hurled him into their midst, scattering them like skittles.

Of course, Tiffany's dad had known for some time he'd been going through some extraordinary physical changes that were connected with the experiments he'd been carrying out. And he'd gone to great lengths to conceal them from the rest of his family by doing things like buying XXL sizes in shirts, trousers and pyjamas, and avoiding family swimming sessions. However, until he charged into that mob of freakish creatures, which he'd been so instrumental in creating, he hadn't quite realised just how significant these changes were. Now, as he landed a positive pile-driver of a punch on one brute whilst simultaneously drop-kicking another back into the Alpha Birthing Pool, for the first time in his life he knew what it was like to have real physical strength. And it felt good.

Now, 100-per-cent confident of his powers, or as some might say, his 'super-powers', Dr Trotter waded into the hideous horde, his fists windmilling, his elbows going like pistons and his feet thrashing, time and time again. And, no matter how savagely his appalling creations bit, tore, punched and scratched him, he seemed completely immune to their assaults. Over and over again, their blows bounced off his rock-solid abdomen, their teeth broke on his bulging biceps and their fists shattered on his stunning quadriceps. And, as he stood up to their batterings, giving back twice as good as he got, it occurred to Dr Trotter that, in his quest to find that elusive 'invincibility' gene, he had somehow given it to himself.

Some thirty minutes later, after a furious battle in which heads were broken, bones crunched and freaks rendered permanently out of action, the whole gruesome bunch lay at the scientist's feet.

'Hmmm,' Dr Trotter said to himself, wiping away a smear of blood. 'Not bad for a nerdy wimp, even if I say so myself!'

However his troubles were far from over. The scientist now felt something cold and metallic being pressed hard against his temple. It was the barrel of Professor Perfidious's pistol.

'Twotter, you blinking wotter!' snarled the professor, apparently oblivious to the fact that Dr Trotter had just saved his life. 'You have wecked my gweat plan. You have betwayed me. And you know what I said would happen if you did that, don't you?' Then he reached into his pocket, pulled out his mobile and held his thumb over the 'send' button, which would instantly transmit the instruction to Zoltan, Cholera and Pancreas to wipe out Dr Trotter's family.

'Yes, Twotter!' snarled Professor Perfidious, an evil grin spreading across his bony face. 'Just as I pwomised, your family are now going to quite misewably and howwibly die! And, once I have welished watching your sowwow bought about by that twagic occuwence, you, too, are going to pewish!'

'You're hideous, Perfidious!' yelled Dr Trotter, beside himself with rage. Then, even though he knew for certain that he wasn't immune to bullets fired at point-blank range, he threw himself at the professor.

The first bullet missed Dr Trotter. But the second smashed into his hand, causing him to yell in pain as he knocked both pistol and mobile from the madman's grasp.

The pistol fell at Dr Trotter's feet, enabling him to sweep it up with his good hand. But the mobile bounced away, its 'send' button hitting the floor hard. Despite his heroic efforts, Dr Trotter knew for certain that the fatal text message had just been sent and there was nothing he could do to stop it. He felt his heart shatter into a million pieces.

CHAPTER FOURTEEN

It was now extremely overcrowded in the rusty old black van. Tiffany and Nigel Redbridge were on the front seat, squashed between Zoltan and two slobbering Rottweillers. Mrs Trotter and Toby were sitting behind, a Rottweiller between them, and Cholera and Pancreas squeezed in at either side. And then there was Marbles.

Kerchung-ping-twattle-twattle-ping! went Zoltan's mobile. He grunted, reached into his pocket, took it out and began to read:

```
Darling Fizzy Pips, forgive my last
text. My relationship with the person
I mentioned is over. She's just told
me  she  thinks  I'm  a  pompous  twit.
Oh dear, what have I done? Please,
please take me back. Yours for ever,
Sherbert Fountain XXX
```

Zoltan looked puzzled. Then he saw it wasn't actually his mobile he was looking at, but Tiffany's. He had taken it from her pocket by mistake, thinking it was his. He handed it to her with a shrug.

Tiffany took it from him and read the message. Then, after briefly typing in an answer:

```
Get lost, Sherbert! Of course you're
a pompous twit! Yours no longer,
Fizzy Pips
```

she pressed 'send' and turned to Nigel Redbridge, giving him a look one hundred times more warm and affectionate than any she'd ever given Julian.

Kerchung-ping-twattle-twattle-ping! This time it *was* Zoltan's mobile. He reached into his pocket, took it out and read the text message:

```
Trotter has betrayed me! Eliminate
his wife and children immediately!
And the pony! Professor Perfidious.
```

The moment the gun was knocked from his hand, Professor Perfidious had made a dash for the conference room door. However, Dr Trotter had beaten him to it and was now standing there, blocking his escape route. He twirled the pistol and coldly regarded the person he now hated more than anyone on Earth.

A year ago, if anyone had told this decent, kind and gentle man that one day he would seriously consider taking the life of another human being, he would have laughed in their face. Now, aware that this lunatic was responsible for the murder of his entire family, not only was he about to do that very thing, he was also looking forward to it. And Professor Perfidious knew it, too.

'Please weconsider, Twotter!' he begged, tears of terror trickling down his cheeks.

But Dr Trotter shook his head.

The rusty old black van came to a halt in the car park of IFARTFASTA. A moment later, its occupants climbed out and began to make their way towards the Alpha Birthing Unit.

Professor Perfidious was now grovelling at Dr Trotter's feet, sobbing uncontrollably and begging his forgiveness. 'I'll give you anything, Twotter,' he wept. 'Anything you ask!'

But Dr Trotter remained silent, his eyes narrowed and his mouth set firm. Then he took careful aim at a spot between the professor's eyes and began to squeeze the trigger, knowing that in the next instant he would be blasting his tormentor to who-knows-where.

'Please, Dr Twotter, please don't –' whimpered Professor Perfidious.

Wham! went the conference room door.

'Hmmmph!' went Dr Trotter, as it hit him squarely between the shoulder blades, knocking him off his feet and sending the pistol skidding across the floor.

Tiffany came stumbling through the doorway and looked around the room. 'Dad!' she gasped, hardly recognising her muscle-bound father.

'Thomas!' gasped Mrs Trotter, clapping a hand to her mouth, as she looked at her husband's sweat-stained body and bloody hand.

'Daddy!' squealed Toby, breaking from his mother's grasp and scampering over to Dr Trotter.

'Yesssss,' snarled Professor Perfidious picking up the pistol, but then almost dropping it again as he saw Zoltan, Cholera, Pancreas and Nigel Redbridge come rushing into the room.

'What the –?' he gasped, looking as if he'd seen a ghost. But then the madman's all-powerful instinct for survival took over. In a flash, he reached for little Toby and scooped him up in his arms. Then, pressing the gun to the terrified child's head, he barked, 'OK, no one move, or the bwat gets it!'

'You wouldn't!' gasped Dr Trotter, hardly believing his ever-changing fortunes.

'Oh yes, I would,' hissed Professor Perfidious. 'Now, all of you. Out of my way. The bwat's my ticket to fweedom!'

But he was wrong. This time, rather than screaming in terror at being in the arms of this ghoul, Toby sank his teeth into his assailant's hand.

'Aaargh!' shrieked Professor Perfidious.

'Nice one, Toby!' yelled Tiffany. 'Way to go!'

Still yelling with pain, the professor dropped Toby then desperately tried to force his way out of the room.

But the Trotter family was on him like a shot. As Mrs Trotter pulled her son out of harm's way, Tiffany deftly spun on her heel, high-kicking the pistol from the professor's hand in a such a perfect textbook move that Zoltan and his mates gasped in admiration. Then, like a missile blasting from its launcher, her dad's right fist struck the professor on the side of his head. Next it slammed into his jaw, lifting him into the air. A second later, he landed at Tiffany's feet, out cold.

'Serves you right, Prof. That's what you get for messing with my dad,' she said proudly, giving him a couple of firm taps with her foot, just to make sure he was well and truly out of action.

EPILOGUE

When that very rusty old black van had pulled up next to her, Mrs Trotter was simply hoping for someone to give her and Toby a lift to Trowser's Down village. Of course, she had realised from all that barking, snarling and terrified screaming that something a bit out of the ordinary might be taking place inside it. But nothing had prepared her for what followed.

The first thing that had happened was a very large, tattooed man, his IFARTFASTA security uniform torn and ragged, had literally fallen out of the van. He was closely followed by a huge, snarling Rottweiller that was obviously intent on causing him maximum harm.

Next, the back doors of the van had burst open and two more security men tumbled out, their clothes also ripped. They, too, were closely followed by a pair of ferocious Rottweillers that were also obviously very keen to sink their fangs into the men's flesh.

Recognising a dominant dog/helpless human situation if ever she saw one, Mrs Trotter instantly went into professional dog-whispering mode. Making sure Toby was out of harm's way, she put herself between the snarling Rottweillers and the sobbing security men. Then, just as she had done so many times before, she quickly worked her magic on the three drooling beasts. She also did quite a good job on the Rottweillers. Just two minutes later, both the dogs and the security men were eating out of her hand.

The three 'tough guys' then threw themselves at Mrs Trotter's feet, thanking her for saving them from the dogs which, as Zoltan explained, had been 'nuffin' but aggro' since the day Professor Perfidious had put them in their charge. Then, much to Mary's amazement, all three of them began begging her forgiveness for the terrible things they assured her they had no intention of doing to the Trotter family, even though they were half-expecting a text from Professor Perfidious telling them to go ahead with those things at any moment. And, just to prove they were telling the truth, they related the true story of what had happened to Dr Redbridge and her family:

Having been instructed by Professor Perfidious

to eliminate the Redbridges in as painful a way as possible, the trio of would-be torturers had discovered they could no more harm them than they could say 'boo' to a Rottweiller. So, having got the family to supply the appropriate ghastly sound effects, they had *pretended* to do horrible stuff to them, safe in the knowledge that the professor would hear the awful noises and be satisfied that his instructions had been carried out.

Then they had smuggled them out of the Transmutation Chamber at IFARTFASTA to one of ancient ruined barns on Trowser's Down, making them promise to lie low, until the three guards could decide what to do next.

And the grateful Redbridges had done exactly that. However, despite their promise, young Nigel just couldn't resist the temptation to nip out and give his new golf clubs a whirl. Which turned out to be very lucky for Tiffany.

Now, much to Julian Butternut's despair, the two of them had become very close friends indeed. And with Professor Perfidious permanently locked away, IFARTFASTA was re-opened under new management. Once more working alongside Dr Trotter, Dr Redbridge resumed her research duties at the laboratories. She and her family moved back into Crumbling Cow Cottage and the Trotters moved into a house just down the road from them. Which of course meant Tiffany and Nigel could spend lots of time together.

Under Tiffany's expert tuition, Nigel soon became an excellent rider, and the two of them would often gallop across Trowser's Down, loving every minute of it. Yet despite all Nigel's efforts, Tiffany could never get the hang of swinging a golf club. Or understand why so many people saw it as such a fun thing to do. However, thinking back to that unforgettable meeting with Robert and Roseanne, she could see that being able to hit those hard little balls with such great force and pinpoint accuracy could occasionally come in quite useful!

Also by Michael Cox...

DYING TO MEET YOU

"Enough is enough, I'm going to get help..."

Twins Hailey and Hugo Huckleberry have
won the prize of a lifetime – the chance to meet
their favourite horror author, Chad Piranha.
Accompanied by Chad's editor, Tamara,
they set off for his solitary mountain hideaway.
But little do they suspect the series of
blood-chilling events that are in store...

Black Cats
Books to pounce on

More Black Cats...

The Gold Spectre • Elizabeth Arnold
The Ramsbottom Rumble • Georgia Byng
Time and Again • Rob Childs
B.A.S.E. Camp • Rob Childs
Footsteps in the Fog • Terry Deary
Into the Lion's Den • Terry Deary
Bryony Bell Tops the Bill • Franzeska G. Ewart
Under the Spell of Bryony Bell • Franzeska G. Ewart
Bryony Bell's Star Turn • Franzeska G. Ewart
Billy Angel • Sam Hay
The Spoon of Doom • Sam Hay
100% Pig • Tanya Landman
Planimal Magic • Rebecca Lisle
Eyes Wide Open • Jan Mark
The Gods Are Watching • Caroline Pitcher
James and the Alien Experiment • Sally Prue

Black Cats
Books to pounce on

More Black Cats...

Changing Brooms • Sue Purkiss
Spook School • Sue Purkiss
Spooks Away • Sue Purkiss
Cry in the Dark • Dee Shulman
Big Iggy • Kaye Umansky
I am a Tree • Kaye Umansky
I Live in a Madhouse • Kaye Umansky
Galaxy Patrol • Jean Ure
The Honourable Ratts • Karen Wallace
Quirky Times at Quagmire Castle • Karen Wallace
Something Slimy on Primrose Drive • Karen Wallace
Drucilla and the Cracked Pot • Lynda Waterhouse
Arf and the Happy Campers • Philip Wooderson
Arf and the Tarantula • Philip Wooderson
Moonmallow Smoothie • Philip Wooderson

Black Cats
Books to pounce on